Anybody Home?

by Marianne Berkes

illustrated by Rebecca Dickinson

Polly 'Possum needed a home. She looked up at the busy oak tree. Was there room for her?

As Polly climbed up the tree, she stepped on something sticky.

"Hey, watch it," said Sammy Spider. "I just finished spinning my web. I don't need you messing it up."

"You live here?" asked Polly.

"Yes, and it's where I snag my food, but I can't eat you. So, bug off!"

"I need a room," said Polly.

"Robbie Robin has a house up the tree!"

"Was that him with grass in his beak?" asked Polly.

"He uses grass and twigs. I spin silk: dry threads and sticky threads. We all build our homes differently!"

"I'm not a builder. I'm looking for a place to rent."

"Well, good luck," said Sammy, checking out an insect caught in the sticky part of his trap.

"Anybody home?" asked Polly.
"Shoooo!" Robbie trilled. "Our babies are hatching!"

"I'm going to have babies too."
"We built our nest way up high to keep predators like you away!"

Just then Becky Bee buzzed by. "Maybe she can help me," thought Polly.

"Anybody home?" asked Polly.

"My, yes," answered Becky. "Lots of us live together in our hive. We store pollen and honey in combs, and we take care of our queen who lays lots of eggs."

"It's a honey of a home, but I don't need to live with any queen," said Polly.

"Maybe you should try Suzy Squirrel's drey down a ways," suggested Becky. "She may still be gathering nuts, but she'll be home soon."

Polly sat on a rock and waited for Suzy Squirrel. Timmy Turtle poked out his head. "You're sitting on my house."

"Oops," said Polly. "What are you doing in there?"

"I carry my home on my back," explained Timmy. "The shell is part of my body and I move wherever I want. I go inside to hide from bad weather and to protect myself from the likes of you!"

"I won't hurt you," said Polly. "I'm looking for a home."

"Go down to the pond," suggested Timmy. "Those busy beavers are always repairing their house. Maybe they'll have a room."

On the way to the beaver dam, Polly saw something moving in the ground. "Anybody home?"

"Go away," shouted Milton Mole. "I need to finish the last room in my burrow before it gets too cold."

"It's still summer," said Polly. "You're making a mountain out of a molehill. Anyway, would you have a room for me?"

"I do have many chambers. I even store food in some," answered Milton, slurping up an earthworm that had fallen through the roof of his tunnel.

"I'll eat almost anything," said Polly, "but digging underground isn't for me. Thanks anyway!"

"Anybody home?" Polly called across the pond.

"We sure are," answered Betty Beaver, "but we have a moat around our lodge to keep critters like you away at night."

"Forget this!" thought Polly. "I'm kind of a night owl, but I don't want to swim to get to my home!"

As Polly headed for the busy tree, a fox ran by. Polly immediately threw herself on the ground and pretended she was dead. Luckily, Freddy Fox went right by her into his den. Polly didn't ask if anybody was at home!

It was almost dawn when Polly noticed some bats flying into a cave.

"Anybody home?" asked Polly.

"Scat!" screeched Billy Bat. "It's our bedtime. We've been foraging for bugs all night."

"I need a home," said Polly desperately, as more bats kept flying into the cave.

"I can hang upside-down too," thought Polly, "and I sleep all day, but all that screeching and flitting about would drive me batty!"

It was dawn when Polly arrived at the oak tree. She noticed a nest of twigs and bark lined with dead leaves. Something was moving inside!

"Anybody home?" she asked.

Suzy Squirrel jumped out. "Don't you dare touch my newborns," scolded Suzy.

"I'm having babies too," said Polly, "but they live in my pouch for a while first."

"That's handy," chitted Suzy. "My kits are still naked and blind, so I can't leave them for long to look for food."

"I'd offer to babysit," said Polly, "but I'm really in a pinch right now. It's the wrong time."

"And the wrong place," said Suzy. "Try Woody Woodpecker's hole. I think he's chiseled out all the bugs he can find."

Polly looked up. Woody was flying away!

"Anybody home?" Polly called into the empty hole.

No answer! Polly moved into the abandoned hollow and slept all day.

That night, twelve babies
were born! Whew!

For Creative Minds

Animal Homes

Animals use homes to sleep, to hide from predators, to raise their young, to store food, and even to hide from weather (heat, cold, rain, or snow).

All animals find shelter in or around things that are found in the habitat where they live—living (plants or even other animals) or non-living (water, rocks, or soil).

Some animals stay in one location for long periods of time while other animals might make a home for short periods of time—as long as it takes to raise young or when travelling.

Animals use dens as nurseries to raise their young. Dens can be burrows, caves, holes, or even small areas under bushes and trees.

Caves protect animals from the hot sun during the day. They also provide shelter from wind and cold weather. Some caves are so deep underground that there is no sunlight at the bottom!

Narrow cracks in rocks (crevices) and tree holes protect animals from larger predators. Most animals can't make crevices bigger but many animals make holes bigger. Once they have a hole big enough, they move in.

A burrow is an underground hole or tunnel. Some burrows have one entrance but other burrows may have many "rooms" and several ways in and out. Once an animal digs a burrow, other animals may move in too. Some animals move in with the burrow-digger. Other animals wait until the burrow is abandoned before moving in.

Many animals build nests with pieces of plants: twigs, grasses, leaves, pine needles, or even mud or pebbles. Birds are not the only animals that build nests. Some reptiles and fish also build nests to lay eggs and to care for their young.

Name the Animal Home

burrow   cave   den   drey   hive

Many spiders weave their homes out of different kinds of thread. Some threads are sticky and will trap prey. The spider knows which threads are sticky and which ones are safe for it to walk on without getting caught in its own trap.

Beavers use their strong, sharp teeth to cut down trees to build dome-shaped homes. To keep large predators away, their homes are often surrounded by water. If the water is not deep enough, the beavers will build dams to raise the water level.

Moles use their sharp claws to dig underground homes with many rooms. The tunnels have several entrances and exits so they won't get trapped by a predator.

Worker bees' bodies make the wax that they use to build small hexagon-shaped cells. The bees attach these cells together to build a home for the bee colony.

When foxes have young, they move into small caves or abandoned burrows. If the old burrow is too small for the fox family, the fox will dig it out to make their new home bigger.

Birds build homes from many different materials. Besides mud, grass and twigs, you might find pine needles, yarn or even a gum wrapper.

Bats live in dark homes that shelter them from light. As they hang from the ceiling, they are out of reach from predators.

Gray squirrels usually use dry leaves and twigs to make their home in the forks of trees.

Box turtles like to bask in the sun, but sometimes hide in cool, wooded areas where they are better hidden from predators. Their home is a permanent part of their body and helps hide and shelter them from attack.

'Possums use the abandoned homes of other animals as their shelter.

hole   lodge   nest   shell   web

Answers: spider web, beaver lodge, mole burrow, bee hive, fox den, bird nest, bat cave, squirrel drey, turtle shell, possum hole

Diurnal or Nocturnal?

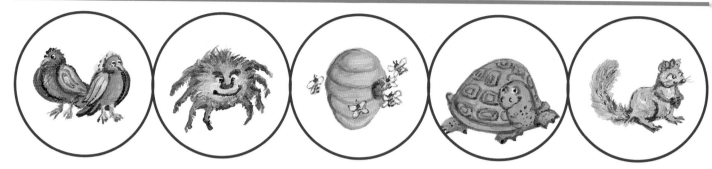

Some animals are active during the day and sleep at night (diurnal). Other animals sleep during the day and are up at night (nocturnal). Sometimes animals that are nocturnal might be seen during the day. For example, Polly 'Possum, carrying her young, had to spend more time looking for food and searching for a new home. Which animals are diurnal and which are nocturnal? Are any animals both?

Robbie Robin gathered twigs and grass for his nest during the day.

Sammy Spider sat in his web all afternoon and into the late hours of the night waiting to catch his prey.

Becky Bee searched all day for flowers rich with nectar and pollen.

Timmy Turtle basked on a log in the warm sunshine.

After scurrying through the trees, Suzy Squirrel returned to her drey before dark.

Milton Mole was busy burrowing both day and night before it got too cold outside.

Betty Beaver piled branches on her lodge in the moonlight.

After hunting all night, Freddy Fox brought food to his family.

Billy Bat returned to the cave to sleep just before the sunrise.

Woody Woodpecker flew away from the hole in the tree before dark.

Polly 'Possum slept in the abandoned hollow all day.

Answers: Diurnal: robin, bee, turtle, squirrel, woodpecker   Nocturnal: beaver, fox, bat, 'possum   Both: mole, spider

Polly's Map

Maps help us to "see" and understand where things are relative to each other. In this story, Polly 'Possum walks around her habitat looking for a new home. She meets different animals and sees their homes. To help us see and understand where Polly went, we can look at a map of the area where she lives.

A compass rose shows directions on a map. Usually maps show the top of the page as north. South is always the opposite of north, so south would be on the bottom of the page. If you look north, east is the direction to your right and west is on your left. Using these direction words helps describe how Polly travels.

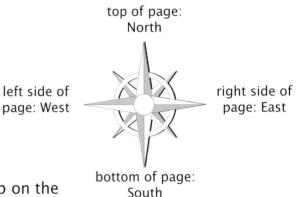

top of page:
North

left side of
page: West

right side of
page: East

bottom of page:
South

Grids give locations on a map. If you look at the map on the next page, you can see that there are red lines crisscrossing over the map. The rows are labeled with letters on the side and the columns are labeled with numbers on the bottom. It's easier to tell someone where something is by using grid coordinates than it is by trying to describe where something is on a map. Using the two maps below, how would you tell someone to find the turtle?

It's easier and more accurate to describe that the turtle is in grid G-10 than to say that the turtle is a little way up the path from the tree, behind the rocks.

Use the map on the next page to:
- Describe the location of the animals and their homes. For example, the turtle is located in grid G-10.
- Describe the directions and number of grids that Polly traveled from one place to another. For example, Polly left the "X" at the tree and has travelled three grids to the east (right).
- Describe the relative location of one home to another. For example, the bats' cave is about 12 grids west (left) of the beavers' lodge.

North/Norte

West/Oeste   East/Este

South/Sur

9 10 11 12 13 14 15 16

With love for the Boyd, Couch, Gainer, Godsoe, Karspeck, McAdam, Meyer, Silware, Vanderslice and Williams families, where I have always felt at home—MB

For Michael Dickinson, thank you for years & years of steadfast friendship and support—RD

Thanks to Jaclyn Stallard, Manager of Education Programs at Project Learning Tree (www.plt.org) for reviewing the accuracy of the animal-home information in this book.

Library of Congress Cataloging-in-Publication Data

Berkes, Marianne Collins.
  Anybody home? / by Marianne Berkes ; illustrated by Rebecca Dickinson.
      pages cm
  Summary: Looking for a new home to raise her expected babies, Polly Possum meets a variety of forest animals and learns how they build and live in webs, nests, hives, shells, burrows, lodges, dens, caves, dreys, and even hollows.
  ISBN 978-1-60718-618-2 (english hardcover) -- ISBN 978-1-60718-630-4 (english pbk.) -- ISBN 978-1-60718-642-7 (english ebook (downloadable)) (print) -- ISBN 978-1-60718-666-3 (interactive english/spanish ebook (web-based)) (print) -- ISBN 978-1-60718-714-1 (spanish hardcover) (print) -- ISBN 978-1-60718-654-0 (spanish ebook (downloadable)) (print) [1. Opossums--Fiction. 2. Animals--Habitations--Fiction. 3. Forest animals--Fiction.] I. Dickinson, Rebecca, illustrator. II. Title.
  PZ7.B45258An 2013
  [E]--dc23
                            2012045032

Lexile® Level: 500L
key phrases for educators: animal/plant interaction, animal homes, life cycles, anthropomorphic, map

Anybody Home?: original title
¿Hay alguien en casa?: title in Spanish
Translated to Spanish by Rosalyna Toth.

Manufactured in China, June 2013
This product conforms to CPSIA 2008
First Printing

Sylvan Dell Publishing
Mt. Pleasant, SC 29464
www.SylvanDellPublishing.com